T0193499

Pandemic Pals

Gabrielle Arron & Gillian Hotz, PhD

Illustrated by Sari Richter

Pandemic Pals

iUniverse books may be ordered through booksellers or by contacting:

iUniverse
1663 Liberty Drive
Bloomington, IN 47403
www.iuniverse.com
844-349-9409

ISBN: 978-1-6632-1295-5 (sc)
ISBN: 978-1-6632-1296-2 (e)

Library of Congress Control Number: 2020922336

Print information available on the last page.

iUniverse rev. date: 11/11/2020

THANKS

I want to thank my human for playing with me, feeding me, loving me and keeping me safe. I love being your roommate.

A big thank you to Marina my dog walker who takes me on fun adventures.

I also want to say thanks to my sister OAKLEY who I miss alot and lives in NYC. I hope she can come visit me soon.

Good morning

My name is Murphy I am a 2 ½ year old Soft Coated Wheaten Terrier.

It is another beautiful sunrise at the beach, however my life has changed a lot. There is a virus called COVID-19 and many things are different.

Let's start with my human! She works from home, on the phone and the computer and makes a lot of noise.

As for me, I get to go on so many more walks now!
They have closed the beaches so I cannot go down near the
ocean. I feel sad because I love playing in the sand.

I am so happy to still be going on my early morning walks.

I see everyone wearing a mask.

I guess it is because of the virus. All humans need to stay safe.

Today instead of going left we went right.
After walking a little we ended up in a new dog park.
The new park is very long it goes from the beach to the street.
I was a little scared because I have never been to this dog park. What if no one wants to play with me?

I ended up playing ball with my human, which was fun.
What I like about this park is there is a tap where I can get water. It was so hot that I rested under the bench before walking home.

The next morning we went to the same dog park.
I looked around the park to see if there were any new pals.
I started running to the park gate off my leash.
I am FREE!!! YEAH.

I saw a big dog running towards me.

My tail began to wag. I was feeling happy.

We played for hours. His name is Raffy and he is a Collie. When Raffy can't slow down he jumps over me. I love my new friend.

Even though we look different, we like playing together.
Raffy has black hair, he is tall and has a long nose and
I have light brown hair, I am short and have a small nose .

It is nice having a new friend. Since the virus came along, I cannot go see my grandma or go to dog school.

Playing with Raffy makes me happy.

I taught Raffy how to drink from the tap.

Sometimes Raffy walks me home after we play in the park.

The next day I was excited to see Raffy again in the park.
I waited and waited but no Raffy. I felt sad, because
I missed my new friend.
I looked to the end of the park.
I saw a Goldendoodle playing.
With my tail wagging, I wondered,
"Who is this new dog?"

Her name is Harley. She is about the same size and color as me but all she wants to do is wrestle.

I don't like to play like that. I miss playing with Raffy.

Maybe I will see him tomorrow?

When I get home, my human wipes my face and paws so I am safe from the virus. I also watch her wash her hands with soap and water.

I am so tired that I fall asleep with my lamby.

I like to go to the new dog park but I miss going to see my friend Trey who is an American Bulldog mix. Because of the virus, I cannot go to Trey's house and play.

We like to play with all the toys and run in the yard.

I am hoping to see him soon.

Sometimes I go to the new dog park before sunset.

I guess all the changes that i was worried about because of the virus are okay. I have new friends and a new park to play with Raffy and a few of our other dog friends. We all have fun playing together!

Sometimes I do wonder when will I go
back and play in my old park.

For now I am happy!

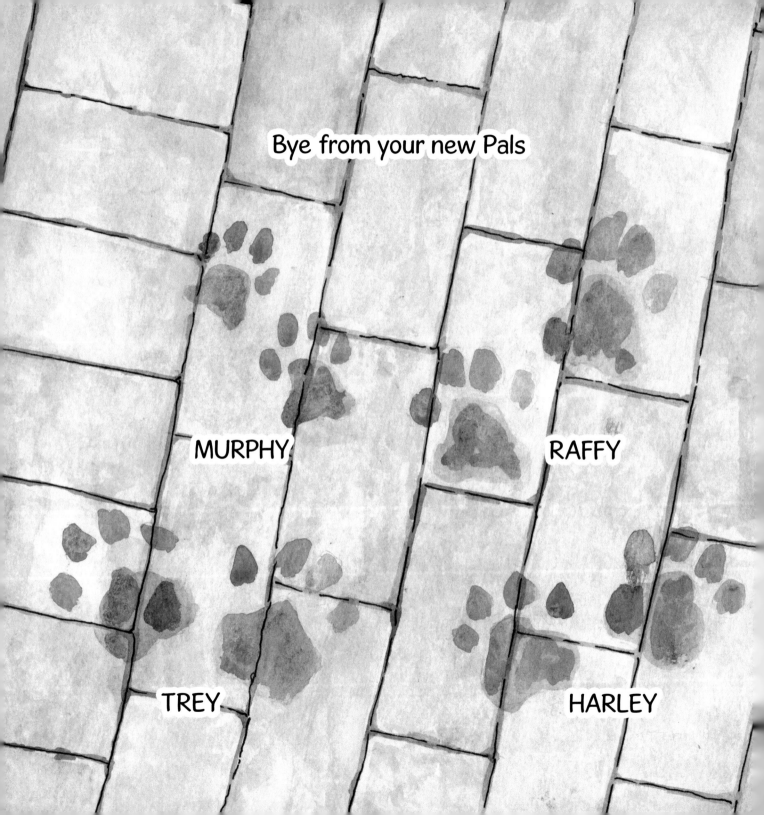

In memory of our family dogs

Tyson

Trigger

About the Authors

Gabrielle Arron is a dog loving 7th grader. She has spent many years raising money for the Berkshire Humane Society and is excited to continue to support them. Gabrielle is an avid reader and writer. During COVID-19 while attending school remotely she was interested in Murphy's new adventures and co-wrote *"Pandemic Pals"*. Gabrielle lives in New York City with her Mom, Dad, Brother Louis and Oakley, who is Murphy's sister from the same litter.

Gillian Hotz, PhD is the Director of the KiDZ Neuroscience Center at the University of Miami Miller School of Medicine. The mission of the Center is to decrease brain and spinal cord injury in children through developing, evaluating and implementing injury prevention programs that educate school age children about walking, biking, skateboarding and playing sports safely. Gillian is also Gabrielle's aunt and lives with Murphy in Miami.

During COVID-19 with all the changes and challenges to Dr. Hotz's busy work schedule. She started working remotely and discussed Murphy's new dog park and daily adventures with Gabrielle sending her pictures of Murphy and her new dog friends. Together they wrote "Pandemic Pals" to document not only the changes in Murphy's life but all human life during these challenging times.

Printed in the United States
By Bookmasters